D1179773

Birthday Gone Wrong

By Meg Greve

Illustrated by Sarah Lawrence

Rourke
Educational Media
rourkeeducationalmedia.com

www.rourkeeducationalmedia.com

Edited by: Keli Sipperley
Cover and Interior layout by: Jen Thomas
Cover and Interior Illustrations by: Sarah Lawrence

Library of Congress PCN Data

Birthday Gone Wrong / Meg Greve
 (Rourke's Beginning Chapter Books)
 ISBN (hard cover)(alk. paper) 978-1-63430-369-9
 ISBN (soft cover) 978-1-63430-469-6
 ISBN (e-Book) 978-1-63430-565-5
 Library of Congress Control Number: 2015933726

Printed in the United States of America,
North Mankato, Minnesota

Dear Parents and Teachers:

Realistic fiction is ideal for readers transitioning from picture books to chapter books. In Rourke's Beginning Chapter Books, young readers will meet characters that are just like them. They will be drawn in by the familiar settings of school and home and the familiar themes of sports, friendship, feelings, and family. Young readers will relate to the characters as they experience the ups and downs of growing up. At this level, making connections with characters is key to developing reading comprehension.

Rourke's Beginning Chapter Books offer simple narratives organized into short chapters with some illustrations to support transitional readers. The short, simple sentences help readers build the needed stamina to conquer longer chapter books.

Whether young readers are reading the books independently or you are reading with them, engaging with them after they have read the book is still important. We've included several activities at the end of each book to make this both fun and educational.

By exposing young readers to beginning chapter books, you are setting them up to succeed in reading!

Enjoy,
Rourke Educational Media

Table of Contents

Chapter One

BFFs

Dear Diary,

I am so excited because my birthday is less than two weeks away! I will be 10, which means I will be double digits! My best friend, Jocelyn, wants to throw a birthday bash for me. Mom and Dad will be out of town again, but they promised a big gift when they get back. I just know Jocelyn and her mom and everyone else will make sure it is the best birthday I have ever had. I feel so lucky that she is my friend!

XO

Kami

Dear Diary,

Kami's birthday is almost two weeks away and I am so excited because Mom said we can throw her a birthday party! I feel really sorry for her because her mom and dad have to be away on a business trip for her special day. I am already making a list of things I need to do:

1. Decide on a theme (Princess? Sleepover? Sports?)

2. Choose food and a cake (Pizza? Tacos? Vanilla or chocolate?)

3. Make a guest list (I am not sure she will want Maria to be there. They had that big fight over the last bit of glitter in art class.)

4. Send out invitations (decide on theme first!)

I really hope she likes everything I plan!

Love,

Jocelyn

When Kami and Jocelyn got to school that morning, they grinned at each other then went to opposite sides of the classroom. Their third-grade teacher, Mr. Perez, decided at the beginning of the school year that they could not sit together. Neither one could stop talking to the other all day, every day. Mr. Perez had even called their parents and told them that the girls were a distraction. Kami and Jocelyn got in big trouble at home. They also had to change seats in class, which was a bummer.

Jocelyn and Kami met when they both fell into a puddle at their favorite park way back when they were both little three year olds. They laughed and splashed until they were covered in mud. That mud bath made them best friends forever. They do everything together, but they don't always like the same things. Kami is messy and unorganized. Jocelyn is always neat and loves to plan ahead.

Kami plopped down in her desk then crossed her eyes and looked at Jocelyn. Jocelyn stuck her fingers in her ears and made a fish face. Both girls put their heads down to muffle their laughter.

"All right, girls and boys, let's settle down," Mr. Perez said. "Today, we are going to start a new project. We will be going on a field trip to the City Aquarium in a little less than two weeks." The class cheered and clapped loudly. Mr. Perez frowned and motioned for quiet.

"You will work with a partner to research and learn about your favorite marine animal. The day before the field trip, you will have an opportunity to share what you learned in a class presentation."

"Awww," the students moaned.

"Now, now, it is important for you to know what you are looking at before you get to the aquarium. This field trip is for learning, not playing," Mr. Perez said.

Kami and Jocelyn rolled their eyes at each other. Kami pointed at Jocelyn and pointed back at herself. "Let's be partners," she mouthed.

Jocelyn read her lips, but before she could happily nod at Kami, Mr. Perez continued, "I am going to assign everyone a partner."

Both girls' shoulders slumped. They should have known Mr. Perez would assign partners. He likes to put people together he believes will not be silly and will get their work done. Kami and Jocelyn already knew they would not be partners. The last time he let them be partners, they started giggling so much during their presentation that they couldn't finish. Their parents did not think that was so funny. Neither did Mr. Perez.

"Jocelyn, you and Timothy are partners. Kami, you and Maria are partners," Mr. Perez said.

Jocelyn's mouth dropped open. *A boy? As her partner? Timothy? At least he is smart and works hard. I wonder how Kami feels*, she thought.

Chapter Two

Project Partners— Ugh!

Dear Diary,

I can't believe Maria is my partner for our class project! She was so mean to me last week. It all started when we both reached for the last bottle of glitter. I had it first. I know I did. But she pulled anyway until the bottle slipped out of our hands and crashed on the floor. Maria blamed it on me. There was glitter everywhere. The art teacher made us sweep up during recess and I didn't get to finish my project. Now I have to work on a project for two weeks with her?! Partners—ugh!

XO, Kami

The next day at school, Jocelyn and Kami sat next to each other at lunch. Kami handed Jocelyn a list of girls' names. "Here is the guest list. I left Maria off of it. She needs to tell me she is sorry first," Kami said.

"What do you want your birthday theme to be?" Jocelyn asked. She twisted her long black hair into a neat braid, then tied it with a piece of red yarn.

"How about a pet theme?" Kami asked.

"Everyone can bring their pet to the party."

"Uhhh, I am not sure about that. My mom is allergic to cats. And don't forget, Leslie has a lizard. We don't want that thing at a party!" Both girls shuddered at the thought.

"How about a princess theme? We can wear fancy clothes and tiaras?" Jocelyn said.

Kami wrinkled her nose. "No, I went to two princess parties in the past two months. Let's do something else."

"Sports or a sleepover?" Jocelyn asked. She was starting to get frustrated with Kami. She liked the princess idea the best. Since she was planning the party, she thought she should get to choose.

"Well, I guess a sleepover would be okay," Kami said.

"Since I am having your party at my house, I think we should do a sleepover.

I want to have pizza too." Jocelyn said. "I was also thinking that we should do cupcakes instead of cake. It's easier to eat and it won't mess up my house as much."

Kami frowned a little bit and shrugged her shoulders, but didn't say anything. She was starting to think maybe having Jocelyn plan her party wasn't such a good idea.

Dear Diary,

Kami is really being a pain. I am being so nice to plan her party for her and she is not being helpful at all. I think she should go along with my ideas since I am her best friend. I know what she likes. I wish she would just let me plan it myself. Anyway, tomorrow we start working with our partners. I am not looking forward to it! Partners—ugh!

Love,

Jocelyn

Chapter Three

Fishy Partners

When Kami and Jocelyn saw each other in class the next day, they waved, but didn't say anything. Mr. Perez had rearranged the students' desks so that the research partners sat next to one another. Kami decided she needed to work out how she was going to get along with Maria for the next two weeks. She didn't want her at her party, but she didn't want to fight with her either. Maria rolled her eyes at Kami as she walked up.

"Hi Maria," Kami said. "I think I need to say I am sorry for last week. I was a little excited to use the glitter."

"Me too," Maria said. "I think I still have

some of it in my desk!" The girls giggled and smiled at each other.

Timothy mumbled and sat down in his desk next to Jocelyn. She tried to scoot her desk a little bit away from his without him noticing. Jocelyn looked over at Kami. She was laughing and talking with Maria.

I can't believe she is being so friendly with Maria. I hope she doesn't think we are going to invite her to her party, Jocelyn thought. The *guest list is already made.*

Mr. Perez told everyone to begin working on their research projects. The students were supposed to look through a few books to choose an animal that was the most interesting to them.

"Do you want to research whales or dolphins?" Jocelyn asked.

Timothy's eyes lit up. "I don't really like either of those animals. How about a sea

turtle, or an eel?"

"Eww, not an eel." Jocelyn said. "They remind me of snakes, and I can't stand any kind of reptile!"

"Eels are not snakes or reptiles. They are pretty cool actually," Timothy said, narrowing his eyes at her.

"Whales and dolphins are such popular animals. Everyone likes them. Which one do you want to choose?" Jocelyn asked again.

"I guess dolphins," Timothy said. He looked a little upset, but Jocelyn decided that since she was stuck with him as a partner, she should get to choose the animal. Plus, it is always *ladies first*, right?

As Timothy and Jocelyn walked over to the classroom library to get some books for their research, Jocelyn noticed that Kami and Maria seemed to be enjoying working together. They were talking and sharing their books as they wrote their notes down.

"Hi Kami and Maria," Jocelyn said. "What animal did you choose?" Jocelyn was trying hard to be sweet and not feel jealous.

"Dolphins," Kami and Maria said at the same time. They looked at each other and laughed.

"Hey, that's what Timothy and I chose." Jocelyn said. She put her hands on her hips.

Maria shrugged. "I guess you have to choose something else," she said. "Mr. Perez said each group has to have a different animal."

"Well, I guess it's an eel then!" Timothy grinned. Jocelyn rolled her eyes and stomped off to the bookshelves.

Why didn't Kami stick up for me? She knows how much I like dolphins. I told her I wanted to be a dolphin trainer when

I grow up, Jocelyn thought. She grabbed a few books about eels and stomped back to her desk. She didn't even look up when Kami tried to talk to her.

Dear Diary,
I had a happy and sad day. Luckily Maria and I are friends again. We had so much fun learning about dolphins today. I am glad I told her I was sorry. But Jocelyn seems really upset with me. I don't know why. I wish she would talk to me and tell me what is wrong.
Love,
Kami

Dear Diary,
I do not like eels!
XO,
Jocelyn

Chapter Four

Partner Blues

For the rest of the week, Jocelyn and Kami hardly spoke to each other. Jocelyn sat with some kids from soccer, and Kami sat with Maria. The two of them laughed and whispered. Seeing them made Jocelyn's stomach feel like it was twisting in knots.

The good part was that working with Timothy didn't turn out to be as bad as Jocelyn thought. *Eels are pretty cool after all*, she thought to herself as they worked. The bad part was that her mom told her the party plans needed to be finished right away. But now Jocelyn didn't even know if Kami was planning to come to her own birthday party!

Jocelyn decided she had to talk to Kami at recess.

"Hi Kami, how are you?" Jocelyn asked.

Kami tucked her long brown hair behind her ear and smiled up at Jocelyn. "I think you've gotten even taller," Kami said.

Jocelyn laughed. "Maybe," she said. "Or maybe you've gotten shorter?" They both laughed at that.

"Want to swing with me?" Kami asked.

"Yes!" They ran over to the swings. When they got there, Kami waved Maria over, too.

When Maria came over, Jocelyn hardly looked at her. *Why can't it just be us*, she thought. Her insides felt hot, like a boiling pot of floppy noodles.

"Hey Kami, we have to finish planning your birthday party," Jocelyn said.

Kami made a surprised face at Jocelyn.

"Yes, I guess we should. Maria, do you want to come to my birthday party?"

"Yes! Thank you so much. I am really excited!" Maria squealed.

Jocelyn couldn't believe Kami. First she didn't want Maria at her party and now she invited her without even asking! The bell rang and everyone galloped back toward the classroom. Kami mixed in with the rest of the students so Jocelyn didn't get a chance to talk to her about Maria.

It was time for more research when

25

they got back in the classroom. Jocelyn told Timothy to get their books and notes.

"I am so tired of you telling me what to do. Stop being so bossy!" Timothy grumbled loudly. He turned and stomped away.

Whoa, Jocelyn thought. She felt her face turn red. She tried to think about what she might have done to make him so mad. *Maybe I have been a little bossy*, she thought.

When Timothy returned with their books and notes, she said, "I am really sorry, Timothy. You are a really good partner and I promise not to be so bossy anymore."

"Thanks," Timothy said, shoving his hands in his pockets. He shrugged and looked at the floor like he was embarrassed. Then he looked up at her with a pretend-serious face. "You have to go get the poster and art supplies then." Jocelyn giggled and went to get the materials.

When she walked past Kami and Maria, Jocelyn ignored them. She didn't know what she was going to do. She was worried that Kami had a new best friend – and her name was Maria.

Dear Diary,

I am so mad at Kami. She invited Maria to her birthday party that I am throwing. She didn't even ask me! I wish I didn't even offer to have the party for her. She is so mean.

Love,

Jocelyn

P.S. Did you know eels aren't really snakes? They are fish!

Dear Diary,

Jocelyn is being so rude. She talked about my party right in front of Maria. I was going to ask Jocelyn in private if I could invite her, but she didn't give me the chance. I kind of wish she wasn't having a party for me.

Love,

Kami

Chapter Five

Shimmery Eels

On presentation day, all of the students in Mr. Perez's class were working hard to get their projects completed. Timothy was in charge of getting the writing done while Jocelyn worked on the poster. They both decided they would make a huge eel on the board. As Jocelyn worked on the finishing touches, she decided the eel skin should look shimmery.

What do I need to make it look shimmery? Glitter! Jocelyn thought. She walked over to the supply table just as Maria got there. They both reached for the bottle of glitter at the same time.

"Hey! Let go! I am using the glitter!"

Jocelyn said.

"I had it first!" Maria said. She pulled a little harder on the bottle.

Jocelyn pulled back even harder. The bottle of glitter slipped and flew up out of both girls' hands. The top flew off, too. The air around them filled with sparkles. The girls shrieked and shouted, "It was her fault!" at the same time.

Mr. Perez walked over to them, a sour expression on his face. "What happened?" He folded his arms across his chest and looked down his nose at them. Both girls tried to explain at once. Mr. Perez clapped his hands, dismissed the class to recess, and handed the girls a broom and dustpan.

Once the class left, the girls started to sweep up. Jocelyn felt a little silly about the glitter, but didn't know what to say. She swept quietly, keeping her eyes on the floor.

Finally, Maria said, "I feel pretty bad about the glitter. It seems like I always have a problem when I want to use it."

Jocelyn looked up at Maria. Her eyes had tears in them. "I am sorry, Maria," she said. "I should have shared. By the way, you have glitter in your hair."

Both girls laughed as they shook their heads to get the glitter out. They finished sweeping up the mess. Then they used some of the glitter from the dust pan on their posters to make them shimmer.

Before the other students came back, Jocelyn said, "Maria, I hope you can come to Kami's party. Do you want to help us finish the plans? I may have been a little bossy with Kami. I really want to make her party turn out the way she wants it!"

"Really? I'd love to help," Maria said. She gave Jocelyn a quick hug. Jocelyn hugged her back and grinned. "I have a really great idea on how we can surprise her," Maria whispered.

Dear Diary,

I felt really silly today when Maria and I fought over the glitter. I know it is better to have more friends, and she really is a nice girl. Maria is helping me with the last of Kami's party plans. She had the perfect idea, too. This is going to be a great party!

Love,

Jocelyn

Dear Diary,

Jocelyn and Maria are friends now!
I am so glad Maria can come to the
party. They both said they have a
surprise for me, but I can't imagine
what it's going to be!

Love,

Kami

Chapter Six

A Glittery Birthday Bash

The day of Kami's party finally arrived. The guests ate pizza, played games, and watched a movie. Finally, it was time to open presents. Kami was so excited to get her gifts. There were dolls, special art paper, and a new diary. Maria and Jocelyn both handed Kami a box.

"This present is actually for all three of us," Jocelyn said.

Kami opened the box and pulled out three T-shirts. Each shirt had three shimmery, glittery letters on them: BFF.

"We thought that since glitter was such a big part of our friendship, we should wear it all the time!" Maria said.

"Just maybe not in our hair," Jocelyn said.

Dear Diary,
Kami's party was so much fun. I loved making a new friend and keeping my old one. This was the best birthday bash ever!
Love,
Jocelyn

Dear Diary,
Jocelyn and Maria had the best party for me. I am so happy we are all friends now!
Love,
Kami

Reflection

Dear reader buddy,

Getting to know Maria and Timothy taught me some stuff about being a better friend. I realized I needed to not be so bossy and give other people a chance to make decisions. Kami really should have been allowed to make her own decisions about her birthday party. And Timothy didn't need me to tell him what to do. Partners work together, they don't boss each other. I also figured out that eels are pretty cool!

XO,
Jocelyn

Discussion Questions

1. Why do you think Jocelyn acted so bossy while she was planning the party?
2. How could Kami have handled Jocelyn's bossy behavior? Should she have kept her thoughts to herself or said something to her?
3. What can we learn from the way Maria and Kami became friends?
4. Can you describe the kind of character that Maria is?
5. Would you want Jocelyn to throw a party for you? Why or why not?

Vocabulary

Make a memory game! Write one vocabulary word on a notecard and write the definition on another notecard. Grab a friend and play memory to practice learning the meanings of the words.

allergic
aquarium
business
distraction
event
invitations
presentation
research

Writing Prompt

Write a diary entry from Maria's point of view to go with the other diary entries throughout the book. What would she say about her friendships and both of the girls?

Q & A with Author Meg Greve

Did you have arguments with friends when you were young?
I did have arguments with some friends, but we always seemed to be able to make up. I learned how important it is to say you are sorry and ask for forgiveness.

What is your favorite birthday party memory?
My mom always planned my parties. They were really fun. We didn't have a lot of money, so everything she did was homemade. That made it seem even more special!

Did you ever have any birthday party disasters?
I remember going to a couple of birthday parties and forgetting the gift or my pajamas if it was a sleepover. I still managed to have lots of fun though.

Party Time!

Plan a fun birthday party with a friend. Even
if it's not your birthday, have a celebration.
Include someone you don't know very well
but would like to be better friends with.

Use Jocelyn's list to make the plan:
1. Decide on a theme.
2. Choose food and a cake.
3. Make a guest list.
4. Send out invitations.

Websites to Visit

Learn about eels:
http://animals.nationalgeographic.com/
animals/fish/electric-eel/

Read more about apologizing:
http://kidshealth.org/kid/feeling/home_
family/sorry.html

Make glitter crafts:
http://kidsactivitiesblog.com/51102/
glitter-crafts

About the Author

Meg Greve is usually a nonfiction author of children's books. In order to write fiction, she had to remember when she was a kid and then change the story to make it more interesting. She played soccer, but never scored a goal, cut her own hair at a sleepover, and had fights with her best friend (but always made up)! Almost all of the story is from her imagination, but some of it has a little bit of truth. Can you guess what it is?

About the Illustrator

Sarah Lawrence always wanted to be an artist, so after graduating from art college in 2006, she took her pencils and started her freelance illustration career. Sarah lives in Brighton (UK), with her daughter, and spends most of her days doodling, drinking tea, and playing princesses.